THE NIGHT BEFORE CHRISTMAS

BY
RICK GEARY

THE NIGHT BEFORE CHRISTMASK™

COLORS BY CHRIS CHALENOR

PUBLICATION DESIGN BY TEENA GORES

EDITED BY MICHAEL EURY AND JOHN WEEKS

THE MASK™ CREATED BY MIKE RICHARDSON

THE NIGHT BEFORE CHRISTMASK™

Published by Dark Horse Comics, Inc.
10956 SE Main Street
Milwaukie, Oregon 97222

ISBN: 1-56971-054-6
First Edition: November 1994

2 4 6 8 10 9 7 5 3 1

Mike Richardson publisher • Neil Hankerson executive vice president • David Scroggy vice president of publishing
Lou Bank vice president of sales & marketing • Andy Karabatsos vice president of finance • Mark Anderson general counsel • Editorial
Diana Schutz editor in chief • Randy Stradley creative director • Bob Cooper editorial coordinator • Bob Schreck group editor: creator-owned titles
Barbara Kesel group editor: legend titles • Michael Eury group editor: company-owned titles • Ryder Windham group editor: licensed titles
Production & Design • Cindy Marks director of production & design • Sean Tierney computer graphics manager • Mark Cox art director
Cary Grazzini senior designer • David Chipps coloring department manager • Richard Powers print manager • Accounting
Chris Creviston director of accounting • Marketing • Michael Martens marketing director • Tod Borleske sales and licensing director

y name's Ned.

T'was the Night before Christmas,
a couple of years back, and I was
miserable.

My parents were out of the city
(I can't exactly remember why),
and I was staying with my Uncle
Stanley in his apartment downtown.

I worried about what Santa would
do when he came by my house and
found nobody there. Who would
think to look for me
in this neighborhood?

Uncle Stanley's heart is in the right place. He tried all evening to cheer me up.

"Don't worry," he said, "Santa finds everyone. You couldn't hide from him if you tried."

Besides, he knew of a special present that would be waiting for me in the morning!

I wasn't quite convinced.

stayed awake that night, after Uncle Stanley went to bed, still worried about Santa.

Santa is getting old, after all, and he must need help these days. (Some of the kids in the neighborhood told me he never comes around.)

Behind me, I heard the creak of a door swaying open...and saw a pair of glowing eyes.

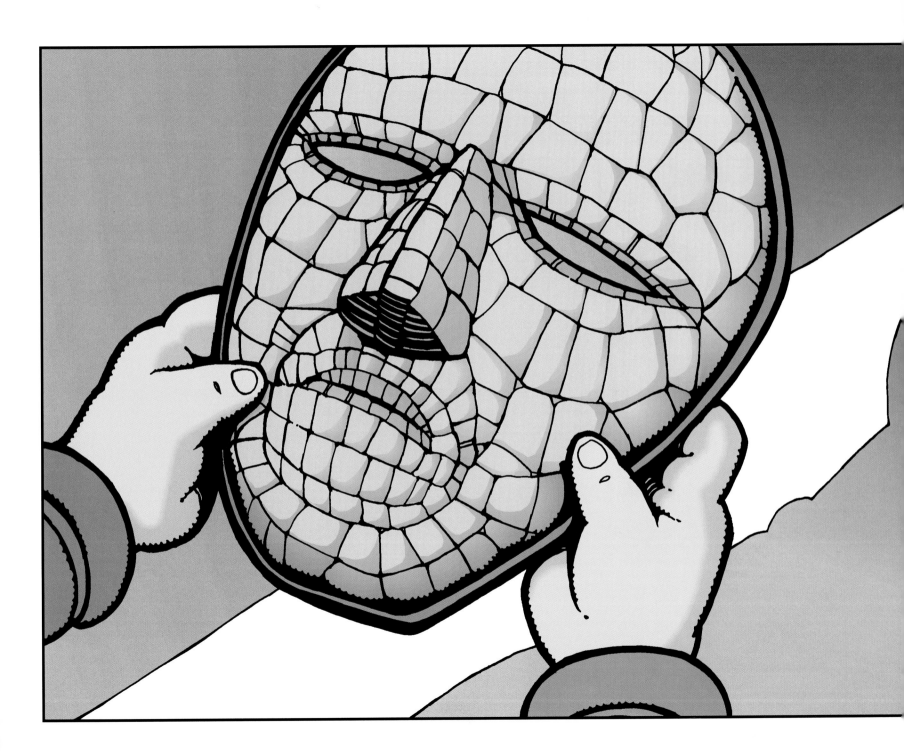

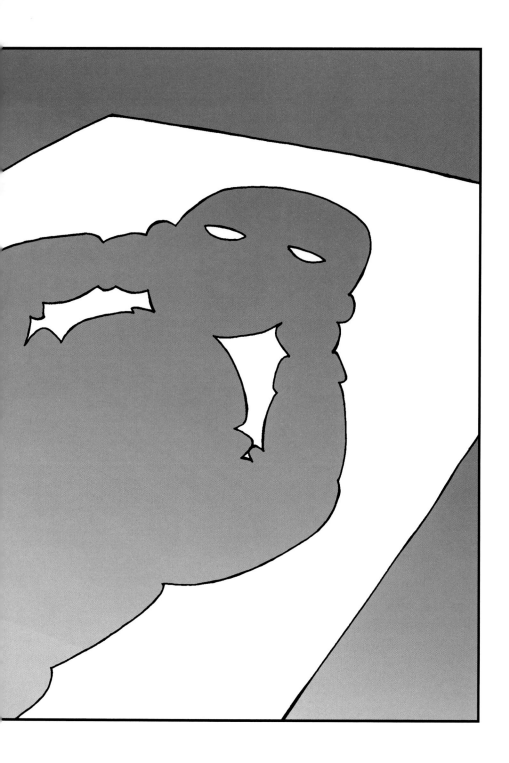

It was a fearsome mask that looked very, very old. Was this my special present?

I could feel it vibrate with a strange power.

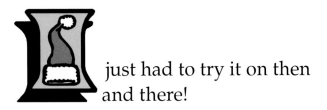 just had to try it on then and there!

What happened next? I'm not sure.

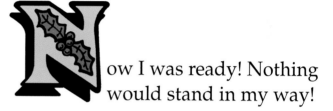ow I was ready! Nothing would stand in my way!

I suppose I wasn't too handsome...but the color of my face matched the season!

With surprising ease, I found the homes of all the kids in the neighborhood, and squeezed down their chimneys.

This Santa job was fun!

I got lucky at the very first apartment! Waiting for me was a glass of milk and an assortment of home-baked cookies...

Also, I soon found out, a fierce and jealous bulldog!

tossed the poor doggie a bone, to keep him occupied while I went about my business.

He found out too late it was made of bubble gum!

At another home, a kid had set up a circle of cameras, hoping, I'll bet, to impress his friends with candid photos of Santa at work.

hat, I wondered, would his friends make of these shots?

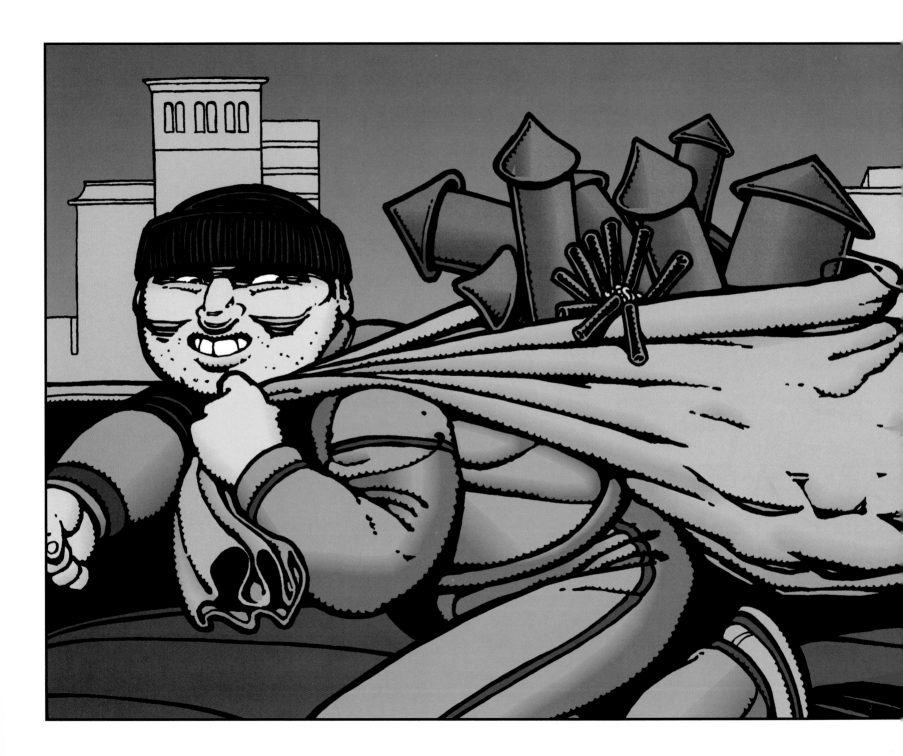

fter a very tiring
evening, I was ready
for bed...

But with just a few more chimneys
to go, my bag was grabbed by a
daring rooftop robber.

Too bad he didn't notice what
was inside!

The sky lit up bright as day!
(Was it Christmas or the
Fourth of July?)

With luck, I found Uncle Stanley's
chimney.

o my surprise, there was Santa...busily arranging a spectacular pile of presents just for me!

He thanked me for my help but added, "Next time don't worry... I always find everybody."

Exhausted but happy, I quietly slipped the mask into his bag and went to bed.

I heard him proclaim as he rode out of sight, "Happy Christmas to all...and don't quit your day job, kid!"